151843

Scatterbrain SAM

Ellen Jackson

Illustrated by Matt Faulkner

🦊 Whispering Coyote
A Charlesbridge Imprint

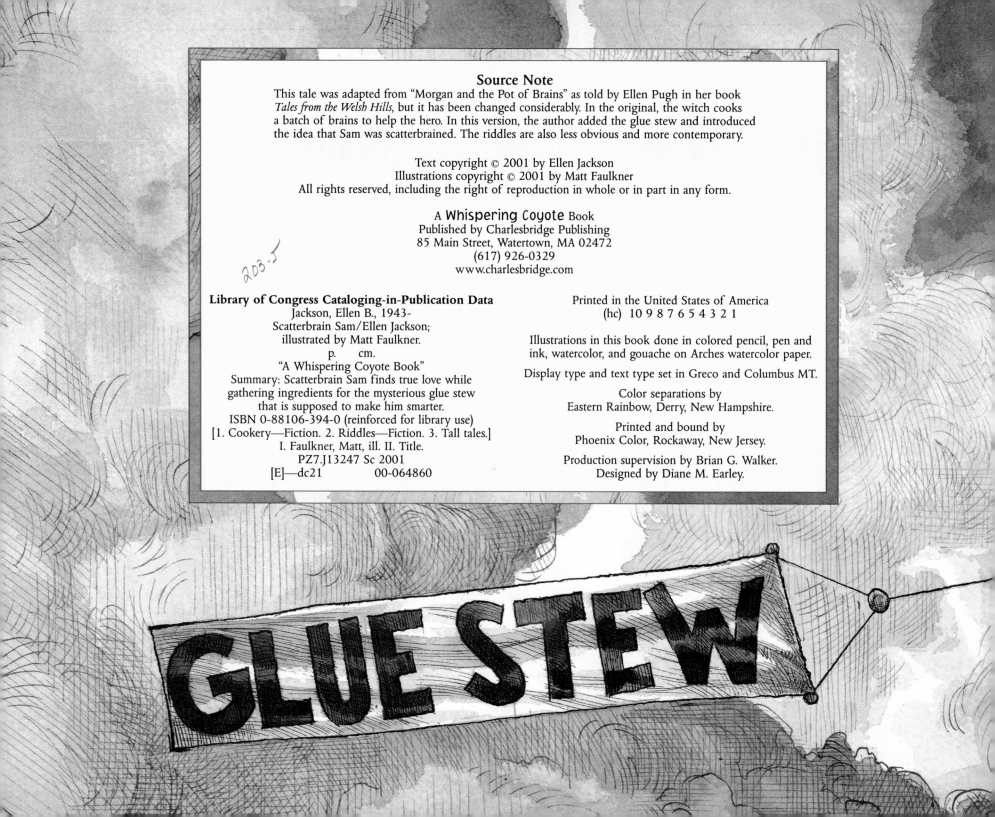

Source Note

This tale was adapted from "Morgan and the Pot of Brains" as told by Ellen Pugh in her book *Tales from the Welsh Hills*, but it has been changed considerably. In the original, the witch cooks a batch of brains to help the hero. In this version, the author added the glue stew and introduced the idea that Sam was scatterbrained. The riddles are also less obvious and more contemporary.

A **Whispering Coyote** Book
Published by Charlesbridge Publishing
85 Main Street, Watertown, MA 02472
(617) 926-0329
www.charlesbridge.com

Library of Congress Cataloging-in-Publication Data
Jackson, Ellen B., 1943-
Scatterbrain Sam/Ellen Jackson;
illustrated by Matt Faulkner.
p.   cm.
"A Whispering Coyote Book"
Summary: Scatterbrain Sam finds true love while
gathering ingredients for the mysterious glue stew
that is supposed to make him smarter.
ISBN 0-88106-394-0 (reinforced for library use)
[1. Cookery—Fiction. 2. Riddles—Fiction. 3. Tall tales.]
I. Faulkner, Matt, ill. II. Title.
PZ7.J13247 Sc 2001
[E]—dc21   00-064860

Printed in the United States of America
(hc) 10 9 8 7 6 5 4 3 2 1

Illustrations in this book done in colored pencil, pen and ink, watercolor, and gouache on Arches watercolor paper.

Display type and text type set in Greco and Columbus MT.

Color separations by
Eastern Rainbow, Derry, New Hampshire.

Printed and bound by
Phoenix Color, Rockaway, New Jersey.

Production supervision by Brian G. Walker.
Designed by Diane M. Earley.

GLUE STEW

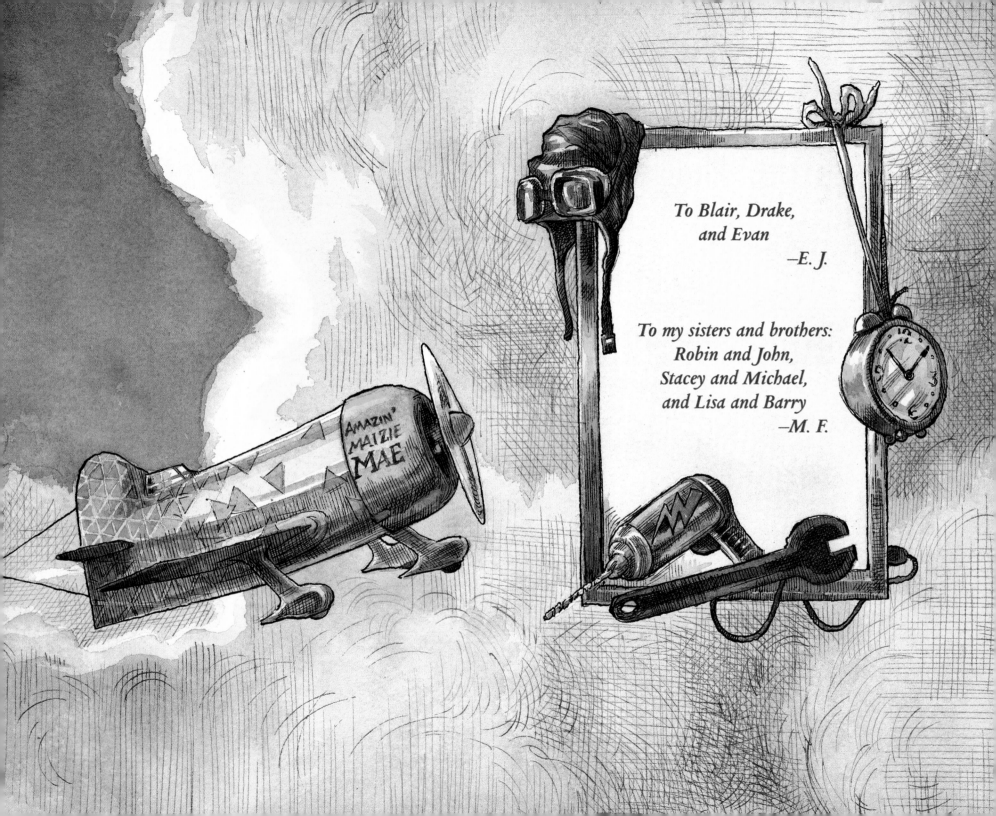

To Blair, Drake,
and Evan

—E. J.

To my sisters and brothers:
Robin and John,
Stacey and Michael,
and Lisa and Barry

—M. F.

Now Scatterbrain Sam was a young fellow who lived all alone on a big farm.

But that Sam—he didn't know nothing about nothing. He kept the hog and the dog in the cellar, and the sow and the cow on the roof. He slept in his Sunday britches, and he ate his soup with a pitchfork.

Well, it wasn't long before Sam got tired of all the buzz-buzz and carrying on behind his back. So he went to see the widder who lived on the hill. Sam had heard tell that she knew about powders and potions and whatnot.

"Widder Woman," said Scatterbrain Sam, "could you mix me up something to fix my brains? They's always pulling this way and that till a fella don't know left from right or right from wrong."

"Hmm," said the widder. She threw some red pepper tea, a wad of string, and a cup of hog lard into a big pot. "I got something that'll fix your noggin, boy. You ever hear tell of glue stew? I'm mixing up a batch now."

"Whoopee!" said Sam. "That'll stick my brains together. Much obliged."

"If I help you, you'll have to help me with the cooking," said the widder. "Bring me something you love to throw in the stew—for flavoring."

So Sam went home and catched hold of Toodles, his canary bird.

"I need you for the glue stew," said Sam. "You been a good bird. I'll be sorry to see you go."

Toodles nestled in his hand, a soft ball of fluff. Poor Sam! How could he drop his little Toodles in that stew?

"Widder Woman," said Sam when he reached the widder's, "here's my bird. But, ma'am, I jest can't bear to think of Toodles cooking in that stew. Ain't there some other way to fix this thing up?"

"Maybe," said the widder. "But you'll have to do some riddling, boy. Here goes: 'Instead of a weed, thar's a song in this seed.' Git me some for the stew."

"That's the riddle?" asked Sam.

"Take it or leave it," said the widder.

Scatterbrain Sam went and sat by the river. He thought long and hard about the riddle, turning it this way and that way, but no ways did it make no sense.

Along came Maizie Mae. That gal had set her cap on Sam. She had seen things other folks hadn't, like the way he fed the birds and the deer in the winter and his kindness to his old mare, Winnie. It wasn't no accident that she was droppin' by for some chitchat.

"Howdy do, Sam," said Maizie Mae. "Can't help but notice that you look a little long in the jaw."

Now Sam never got a thought in his head without it leaking out of his mouth at the first opportunity.

"I'm gettin' my brains together, Maizie," said Sam. "And I got trouble, riddle trouble. This one's a slippery so-and-so. It goes like this: 'Instead of a weed, thar's a song in this seed.'"

"That's the riddle?" asked Maizie Mae.
"Birdseed, I'll wager."

"Whoop-dee-doo!" said Sam. "I believe
you done got it, Maizie Mae. What a gal!"

He went home, got a pinch of birdseed,
and brung it to the widder.

"Maizie Mae helped me figure the riddle," he said. "How're we doing on the glue stew?"

"It's coming," said the widder tossing in the seed. "But it's a little flat. I'll be wanting something else you love in the pot—for savoring."

"That would be—let me see—Sweet Sadie the cat," said Sam with a frown.

So home he ran to fetch Sadie.

When Sam got there, Sweet Sadie jumped in his lap and began to purr. He thought of his dear little kitty bubbling and boiling in the pot of stew. But he picked her up and ran back to the widder's.

"Ain't there some other way, Widder Woman? She's such a good kitty and a fine mouser, too," said Sam.

"Well, I suppose," said the widder. "But first you got another riddle coming, boy. Here goes: 'A cat with no mew to swim in the stew.' Git me one."

"That's it?" asked Sam.

"Take it or leave it," said the widder.

Scatterbrain Sam went up yonder and sat on Rattlesnake Ridge. He turned that mean ol' riddle in his head this way and that. But no ways did it make no sense.

Then who should come along but Maizie Mae. When Sam saw her he started grinning like a possum in a peanut patch.

"Howdy, Maizie," said Sam. "What brings you to this neck of the woods?"

"Been pinin' for bird nest soup," said Maizie, friendly as ants at a picnic. "Best bird nests in the county right over yonder. So what're you doin' out here all on your lonesome? You got yourself another riddle?"

"Yup," said Sam. "This one's a humdinger. It hurts my head to think about it. 'A cat with no mew to swim in the stew.'"

"Catfish, I reckon," said Maizie Mae.

"Why, Maizie Mae," said Sam, "those brains of yours pull together better than a team of mules!" Off he raced to get some catfish for the widder.

"That glue stew's a sight to behold," said Sam when he reached the widder's. "And here's the catfish, courtesy of Maizie Mae."

"Still, it ain't right," said the widder, giving the stew a stir. "You got something you love you ain't told me about?"

"I dunno," said Sam. "I'll think about it."

Down at the meadow was as good a thinking place as any, being it was sort of sunny-like, so that's where Sam headed. Pretty soon along came Maizie Mae. She was wearing a brand-new splinterfire dress.

Sam looked at Maizie Mae. She was such a friendly gal and smart as a whip. Why, come to think of it, Sam didn't know what he'd do without her.

"What I wouldn't give for a head full of high-class brains like yours, Maizie," said Sam. He took her by the hand and led her to the widder's.

"Widder Woman, I just figured that Maizie's the one I love best. But I ain't about to drop her in the stew."

"Don't be getting cold feet now," said the widder. "Jump in, gal."

Maizie climbed—just to take a gander. The stew was boiling and bubbling away. "I don't reckon," she said.

"Don't you got one of them pesky riddles?" Sam asked the widder. "Maizie Mae can rassle them riddles with one arm tied behind her."

"Plum out of riddles," said the widder.

"Tarnation! Scatterbrain Sam I am, and Scatterbrain Sam I'll stay," sighed the boy.

Just then Maizie sneezed. Some of that red pepper tea was a-tickling her nose. KERPLUNK!

"Maizie!" cried Sam.
Without consulting his brains,
the boy did the right thing—
he tipped over the pot of stew.
    Then that stew took off.
It rushed out of the house,
carrying Maizie along. Down
the hill it charged, gathering
speed. Sam and the widder
ran after it.

"Maizie! Maizie!" cried Sam. The glue raced through Jed MacGruder's barn, hanging the barn door back on its hinges and shoeing a couple of horses.

It galloped through the schoolhouse and patched up some windowpanes.

It dashed through town where it mended the cracks in the sidewalk. It stuck the stamps on the letters at the post office and put them in the box for good measure.

Finally it came to rest with a sizzle and a snort. Sam found Maizie glued to the church door.

"You're safe," he said wiping her off. "But shucks, I'll never get my brains gathered together."

"You got some brains gathered together, boy," said the widder. "Hers."

"But what about the glue stew?" asked Sam.

"It worked, son. That gal's sticking with you like flies to honey. Take her up to the preacher and marry her before she thinks better of it."

And that's just what he did.